DAY 1 - Tuesday, May 27 - [12:15am]

Sometimes I get these strange feelings. Do
you ever meet someone and get a feeling
about them? And not in a creepy way - just
the thought that maybe you met before even
though you know you haven't? I get these
feelings sometimes. And I got a feeling
about you when I saw your Instagram page
today. It felt like maybe I should write to
you. I don't know. It's just a feeling.
But once in a while I think things are going
to happen before they do. Does that ever
happen to you? Like maybe you open the door
before someone knocks. Anyhow, thanks for
checking out my writing and liking my posts
today. I'm glad I looked at your profile.

DAY 1 - Tuesday, May 27 - [12:37am]

Also, I noticed we live in the same
neighborhood. That's cool but I'm not in
Brooklyn right now. Tonight, I am in a
hotel room in the Midwest. My friend is
very sick and I came to try and help. But
I don't feel very helpful. I feel like
I'm just getting in the way. I'll try and
explain more later. Anyway, thanks for
following me on Instagram today, Eileen.
I'll write you again tomorrow.

DAY 2 - Wednesday, May 28 - [1:02am]

My father is 57 years old. Today, after
visiting my friend in the hospital, I rode a
mountain bike with my father through trails
in a forest preserve. My father and I are
not very close. We didn't say much. Still,
it was nice to go on a bike ride together in
the woods. We've never done something like
that before. At least not since I was a
little kid. I think it helped that we were
concentrating on riding up very steep hills,
feeling the earth under us and smelling the
wind blow between the trees. It doesn't
matter what kind of a person you are when
you are in nature. When people shut up for
a second, spirituality and 'the unspoken
truth' takes over and even people who don't
get along realize that deep down, they are
the same.

DAY 3 - Thursday, May 29 - [3:08am]

Eileen, I am very tired and it is late and I
have to fly back to New York in three days.
I have had 6 gin-and-tonics and a bottle of
wine. I am in a town where a lot of people
know me. Someone stopped me in the men's
room tonight and talked to me for a half-
hour about vinyl production and a rock show
that I played at 8 years ago. Eileen, I
know it's not polite for me to say so but

I just want to get back to Brooklyn where I
can walk down the street and be invisible.
I just want to go to the bar down the street
from my apartment and have a drink without
being bothered.

DAY 4 - Friday, May 30 - [10:18am]

I woke up at 6 o'clock this morning and my
entire hotel room was covered in red wine.
It was on my shoes and my suit jacket. It
was all over the bed and on the floor.
It looked like it was raining cabernet
sauvignon. I couldn't find my corkscrew
last night. I vaguely remember calling room
service but they didn't have one either. So
I slammed the cork down into the bottle with
a pen. I was able to drink the wine but
only after it sent a red explosion up onto
the ceiling and sprayed all around me in a
20-foot radius. I guess I'll keep an eye
on my credit card statements to see if they
charge me for the sheets.

DAY 5 - Saturday, May 31 - [12:46am]

Eileen, I had a long drive today. I do not
feel well. My friend Jake is dying. A lot
of our friends keep asking me how he's doing
or how I'm doing and I'd rather talk about

something else. How long have you been an
actress? I like all your Instagram photos
where you're doing flips and hanging from
ropes. What is that called? Trapeze? How
long have you been doing trapeze? How did
you find me on Instagram? Did you read
one of my books? There's something about
you, Eileen. Maybe I could write you for
100 days and send it to you as a book. I
believe that an artist should have a small
audience in mind when creating something. I
think it's best to write something just for
one or two people. When an artist creates
something with "mass appeal," it's usually
shitty. The art turns out soulless. It has
no life. I think when you make art for a
single person just out of reach, it can make
for some pretty special results. Anyhow, I
thought about all of this on my long drive
today.

DAY 5 - Saturday, May 31 - [1:16am]

Eileen, I looked at more of your trapeze
photos today. Those are really amazing. I
like the one where you are in the air with
your arms out. Did you learn how to do that
for an acting gig? Or maybe acting is your
focus and you do trapeze for fun? Who is
the blonde girl in the earlier pics? Is
she your best friend? I don't really like
heights. I prefer to be on the ground. I

think acting is drastically different from writing - at least the kind of writing that I do. I don't pretend to be anyone but myself. I don't think I could ever work with a director. I would get annoyed being told what to do. I'm very stubborn, Eileen. I would never break character. I don't stop writing unless I need to. But my deciding factor is usually rent. I'm like, "Rent is due. I guess it's time to publish that book."

DAY 6 - Sunday, June 1 - [1:55am]

Eileen, I'm doing the best I can out here in the Midwest. I show up. I fight some heavy emotions and pretend to be hopeful. I never let Jake see me sad or scared. It's all I can do. I just keep pushing my emotions down in my throat so my friend doesn't get upset. And then as soon as I get outside in the parking lot, it all comes rushing out in tears and shakes like I'm some sort of babbling lunatic. And then I go straight to the bar. But there's no use talking about it now because I seem to be getting pretty worked up if I think about it too much. I will mourn my friend when he is gone but for now I will keep it together and be a source of support. Eileen, do you ever think that maybe sometimes we can be more honest with strangers than with the people we love?

DAY 7 - Monday, June 2 - [1:46am]

Hey Eileen,
I am back in Brooklyn now. My friend's band
played at Brooklyn Bowl tonight. I was
tired from traveling but it was nice to get
out for a while. I was walking down Wythe
and the sun was setting over the river with
the Empire State Building all lit up in
purple and blue and white. And the sun was
shooting all these deep golden rays against
the warehouses and graffiti. It's quite an
amazing city we live in. I am glad to be
home.

DAY 8 - Tuesday, June 3 - [2:31am]

Hi Eileen,
Tonight I spent some time editing a poetry
book I wrote. It's almost done. And I have
the cover designed already too. I just need
to save money for the printers. It seems
like I'm always trying to save money for the
printers. Still, I sit in my apartment,
typing away and hoping that somehow my
stories will carry me out of here.

I had dinner with friends tonight but
everyone was in a weird mood. And afterward
I even ran into another friend on the street
who is usually an upbeat guy but he didn't
smile as much as he normally does. Maybe

I'm still used to the Midwest politeness
after being there this week. Even the
people on the train seem to be frowning.
I'm doing okay. I'm worried about Jake
but tonight I just blasted 90's music in
my headphones and went looking for a liquor
store that stays open late on Sundays.

Tomorrow I'm going to go to my meditation
group. It's like a punk rock meditation
group. Everyone has a lot of tattoos and
talks about all the drugs they used to do.
I fit right in. We sit there and meditate
in Greenpoint and then the group organizer
talks for a little bit about a topic related
to Buddhism. Eileen, I've been studying Zen
Buddhism for many years. I'm so good at
letting go, I even let go of Buddhism.

DAY 9 - Wednesday, June 4 - [2:30am]

I spent more time working on my poetry book.
I don't think what I do is really poetry.
But I figured out that if I label my books
as "poetry" it's very easy to get on the
bestseller list because no one buys poetry
books. So hopefully, I can say, "I have the
best selling poetry book on the internet,"
and people will roll their eyes at me
because really, what kind of asshole says
that about themselves.

DAY 10 - Thursday, June 5 - [1:23am]

Jake's family started this Facebook group
where they send out updates. It's sometimes
difficult to read. But I feel bad when
I don't respond so I've been checking it
every day and trying to leave some positive
comments. I do not feel ready to work
tomorrow. Everybody's got their problems
I suppose. It's best to keep these things
masked in metaphors or songs or stories
or act out other people's drama on the
screen. It's best to turn that turmoil into
something entertaining, because most people
don't want to deal with the rawness of life.

But all I can think about is Jake laying
in his hospital bed. He keeps texting
me pictures of whale sharks. When I was
visiting him, he said he always wanted to go
snorkeling with whale sharks. They are the
biggest sharks in the ocean and they come
right up to the surface. They feed in Isla
Mujeres in Mexico and some of them are over
40 feet long.

I told Jake that he would make it out of the
hospital and we would go down to Mexico.
And I told him that those whale sharks are
bigger than my apartment in Brooklyn. He
laughed at that.

DAY 11 - Friday, June 6 - [2:16am]

Eileen, my New York friends dragged me over
to the open mic night at Bowery Poetry Club
tonight. What a pile of shit that was. The
poets all said things like, "I was born free
as a summer breeze." It was truly awful.
They just mumbled words into the microphone
and expected us to come up with the meaning.
One of them yelled things like, "Pancakes,
baseball bat, pot hole, Gemini." It was
all really embarrassing. Some of them you
can tell just aren't functioning well in
society. They have that "uncomfortable with
life" look.

A few of them read their poems with intense
passion and clever rhythm - like a poorly
written performance piece. The audience
didn't know the goddamn difference. The
applause always mirrored the performance,
not the writing. The louder they spoke and
the more grandiose their body language, the
more people clapped. I found it all quite
ridiculous.

But I have to admit, I really liked the
unpublished amateurs. Some of them are so
insane they don't actually read poetry.
They just sort of wander onto the stage and
talk about life in strange ways. They make
every one else in the room uncomfortable. I
think I was the only one smiling. That's

real life. Some of them talk in odd
rhythms. They don't realize how quirky
they are — which makes it really something
to watch — mesmerizing. They are more
beautiful than the professionals.

DAY 12 - Saturday, June 7 - [4:14am]

Eileen, I wonder what would happen if you
and I were in a car together headed for the
great north Appalachians. I think you would
look out the window with a slight smile and
neither of us would say much. I think you
are younger than I am. But I would guess
the only disconnect between us would be our
experiences with top 40 radio and where we
were when the World Trade Center collapsed.
Other than those things, I imagine we'd have
a lot of similar worldly experiences. I bet
we'd meet in the great spiritual void where
neither age nor sex matter.

DAY 13 - Sunday, June 8 - [12:02am]

Eileen, Sometimes I want nothing more than
to take a hip hop dance class so that I can
make YouTube videos where I just freestyle
dance to my favorite songs. But in this
life we have to choose. We have to let some
things go so that we can succeed in other
areas.

DAY 14 - Monday, June 9 - [12:26am]

Eileen, I still want to know about acting.
When you become another person for a film,
how do you let that character go? How do
you fall back into your natural state? Do
humans have a natural state? Or maybe we
are all just empty slates. Is that why
Tom Cruise is so strange? Maybe we're just
the manifestations of the stories we tell
ourselves? Eileen, I hope you are telling
yourself a good story.

I didn't plan on being a writer. One day
a couple of winters ago I just wrote down
some things that I was thinking about and
turned them into a little zine. And they
sat in my closet for 3 months. And then
I was cleaning my apartment and thought I
should get rid of them. I asked a bookstore
if they would try selling some. They sold
out very quickly and people started asking
me to write some more. So I did. If you
would have told me two years ago that I'd be
writing a novel and turning down speaking
engagements I'd have called you a real
joker.

DAY 15 - Tuesday, June 10 - [2:52am]

My neighbor and I got some drinks tonight.
The man is a lunatic. I don't know how much

he gets paid but he sure didn't hesitate
when the bartender offered the premium
whiskey. I stuck with my cheap gin and
tonics. The bartender tried to test me with
a weak one. But later he made a couple of
strong ones when he realized I could hold my
own.

DAY 15 - Tuesday, June 10 - [3:06am]

I just looked at your Instagram. Today you
posted a photo of yourself sipping coffee in
a diner. I hope you had a nice day.

DAY 16 - Wednesday, June 11 - [3:46am]

Hi Eileen,
Today was a hell of a day. I had a lot of
meetings in midtown and things to do for
work. When you work in the music industry,
that means staying out until 2 or 3 in the
morning and yelling at each other over loud
music with a strong drink in your hand. It
must have been 90 degrees this afternoon.
I came home in the middle of the day and
took a cold shower and worked some more in
the air conditioning. I am still behind
after being out of town last week. And then
tonight I was out at another show. Usually,
I work from about 9 to 6. And then late at
night I write books. I write for hours and

hours each night. This is when I come to
life.

DAY 17 - Thursday, June 12 - [12:49am]

Eileen, I had a very good day. I spoke
with Jake's family and he seems to be doing
a little better. His sister posted a lot
of encouraging news on the Facebook group
today. They said he might even be able to
go home for the time being and sleep in his
own bed. I was so happy to hear that. I
took a half day at work and went out for a
drink to celebrate.

While I was on the subway, I was listening
to some music on my headphones. I was
tapping my foot and really enjoying the
album. The train stopped at Union Square
and a large group of little kids walked
on. They were all wearing their school
uniforms and they were incredibly fucking
happy! They must have been Junior High
or older Elementary School kids. There
was this crazy, happy energy everywhere.
I couldn't stop smiling. The kids were
laughing and talking to each other. I don't
know what they were talking about. What do
little kids talk about? They were fully
engaged and laughing and playing games
with their hands. They were just so glad
to be there and when they laughed it was

coming from a place of real joy. There was
a little blonde girl that stuck her nose
up and danced. There was a messy smiling
girl with braces and bad gums. She was
playing some game with her friend. They
were all smiles. You could tell the one
with the braces was going to grow up to be
an artist or an actress and sleep around a
lot and take longer than necessary to finish
college. There was a kid who didn't talk to
anybody and just sat there with his head in
his hand. But he was a good kid and happy
too. He just preferred to be by himself and
observe things. And there were two really
chatty boys who you knew were going to be
in some sort of sales job or do something
that involved wearing a tie. And there were
Jewish kids and black kids and snooty girls
and artsy boys and everybody was getting
along and happy to be themselves.

DAY 18 - Friday, June 13 - [4:48am]

Hello Eileen,
Tonight was magical. You know that feeling
you get when it's 3am and you're at the peak
of your drunk but you're not so drunk to be
messy? You've had just enough to attain
enlightenment and a warm happiness in your
chest. And you're in a cab by yourself
headed home. And the driver speeds through
Manhattan bringing you over the bridge where

you can see all the lights. And the night
is warm enough where you can have the window
down and take in all the smells and sounds
and pulse of the city. And you can look
back on your night with appreciation and
gratitude and a sincere hope for the future.
Tonight was that kind of night.

DAY 19 - Saturday, June 14 - [12:58am]

I started my day walking through the offices
of Kickstarter in Brooklyn. Then I had
a meeting over at VICE down the street.
Then I met with friends and went to a film
premiere. There was an after party and
I even made a couple of new friends. And
Eileen, I know we don't know each other but
I don't have many friends. So the ones I
have mean a lot to me.

Tonight you posted a new photo of you and a
Buddhist monk in the West Village! Eileen,
I can't believe it. Are you Buddhist too?
Eileen, sometimes I wish we could hang out
and talk for a long time where no one would
bother us. When I was younger, I saw this
TV show about a boy who could stop time.
And he would walk around and everyone else
would be frozen. But if he touched someone,
they would become unfrozen too. I used to
think it would be so cool if I could do

that. Eileen, if I could stop time, I would
touch you.

DAY 20 - Sunday, June 15 - [2:20am]

Hi Eileen,
Today was a nice day. I drank fresh
vegetable juice and did yoga for thirty
minutes. But I do a lot of sit-ups
and pushups when I do yoga. I call it
superyoga. Last night I spent the evening
hanging out with a band from Portland.
And also some people who work for a movie
company called Oscilloscope. I'm not sure
if I should be name dropping all these bands
and companies. I think it would be better
if I just make up new names for them. Maybe
I could get sued or something. Eileen,
I never knew that being a writer would be
such a messy business. I never know what to
change. If it were up to me, I would just
write about life exactly as I see it. But
apparently people get angry or upset when
you write about them. Apparently the best
thing to do is fictionalize everything and
never base your characters on real people.
I think that's probably why most books are
pieces of shit.

DAY 21 - Monday, June 16 - [2:49am]

I'm getting really tired of meetings.
Eileen, I want to buy land upstate and live
in the woods. I want to build a cabin out
of a shipping container and start smoking
cigarettes again. Maybe that's why you took
up trapeze. Maybe it's a nice distraction
from acting. Every day I see these pictures
of you and half the time you're doing a flip
or swinging 40 feet in the air. You never
show what's under you, Eileen. Is there a
net under you? There must be a net, right?

DAY 21 - Monday, June 16 - [4:18am]

It's past 4:00AM and I really should sleep.
Most likely I will toss and turn and read on
my Kindle until 5 in the morning. Lately,
I've been having all these vivid dreams. I
keep dreaming that Jake has passed away and
he's talking to me as a ghost. And last
night I dreamt I was ice fishing with him
and he wasn't catching anything. He handed
me the fishing pole and I caught a fish.
Then I caught another and another until I
had enough for both of us. That was a good
dream.

DAY 22 - Tuesday, June 17 - [12:17am]

Eileen, I was sitting at Chipotle eating one
of those vegetarian burritos. And another
guy sat down on a different table across
from me. But he sat facing me. So now,
instead of enjoying my meal and being with
my thoughts, I'm suddenly staring at this
ugly bastard shoving dead steak in his mouth
and wiping grease off his lips.

I'm not a vegetarian but watching this large
mammal devour his food made me consider
becoming a vegetarian. It really got me
thinking about how we have to eat other
living things in order to survive. But
lettuce is alive and corn is alive. Trees
are alive and I think trees are the wisest
form of life on our planet. So this guy is
eating his steak and it reminded me of one
of those nature shows where a lion tears an
antelope to shreds. And it made me wonder.
If we're supposed to be peaceful and loving,
why is the natural order of things so
violent and ugly sometimes? Maybe it just
looks bad but the antelope is actually glad
to have it over with quickly.

It's like when you're a kid and you make
a sand castle on the beach and some jerk
comes and kicks it over. That antelope had
spent years building muscle, getting taller,
growing horns, making friends. He probably

had a pretty good sand castle. And sure, he
ran like hell from the lion because nobody
wants their sand castle knocked down. But
maybe it wasn't so bad. Maybe he got to
start over. Maybe it just looked bad but
it's okay now. I know we have to eat to
live. I hope the antelope and green peppers
don't mind too much, Eileen. I really do.

DAY 23 - Wednesday, June 18 - [3:16am]

Today was a good day, Eileen. I finished
the guts of my new book. That's what they
call the inside pages — guts. I learned
that when I signed a distribution deal. I
found a professional printer and he told me
all about guts. My new book will be about
200 pages. And tomorrow I'm going to work
on the front and back covers. I'm not sure
what cool word printers use for that. Maybe
it's 'face and ass'.

DAY 24 - Thursday, June 19 - [11:10pm]

Hey Eileen,
My goddamn typewriter broke the other
day. I had an appointment down at Gramercy
Typewriter Company to get it fixed. It's
the last typewriter repair shop in the
whole city — maybe the country. That's the

thing about living in New York, they have
everything here. If I was in rural Alabama
and needed to have a typewriter fixed they
would say, "Boy, whatcha got? Shit fer
brains? Why don't you use a computer?"

Anyway, I get this typewriter fixed and I'm
in there banging away on the fucker to test
it out and the repair man says, "You're
the first person I've seen in a while that
actually knows how to use that machine.
Most people just come in here to clean up
old machines to display in their office or
show off in a retail store or something.
"Not me," I said. "I'm here to get work
done."

DAY 25 - Friday, June 20 - [3:57am]

I finished my new book. I've been working
for 18 hours. I'll have to check it one
last time in the morning just to make sure
my blurry eyes didn't make any mistakes.
But I'm sending the thing to the printers
before lunch tomorrow. And then I will
celebrate with wine and art and more wine.
Eileen, did you know I'm going to put out
3 books in a three month period. I don't
think that's normal. I've got dark bags
under my eyes and can never seem to sleep
right. I work a lot. I wonder what the
record is for most books written in a year.

DAY 25 - Friday, June 20 - [4:05am]

Okay, I just checked Wikipedia and the most
novels written in a single year is 23. It
sounds impressive but I bet they were
shitty.

DAY 26 - Saturday, June 21 - [12:54am]

I want to take a trip. I need to get out
of here for a while. My old roommate Doug
moved to Puerto Rico a few years ago. I
haven't seen him since he left. Maybe I'll
go visit him and sleep on the beach. There
is a campground on an island near him. It
used to be used as a U.S. Military base and
there are still explosives everywhere. But
it's got the best snorkeling beaches in
Puerto Rico. You have to break through a
government fence and trespass across this
restricted area to this beautiful beach. I
want to do that.

DAY 27 - Sunday, June 22 - [1:36am]

Eileen, last night I had a dream that Jake
was on fire and I put him out.

DAY 28 - Monday, June 23 - [3:23am]

I had to carry 100 books (a previous book,
not my new one) from the Nassau stop all the
way down to the Wythe Hotel. Books are so
heavy. If you put a bunch of paper together
it basically weighs the same as wood. So it
was pretty much like I was carrying a giant
tree stump down Wythe, jumping in front of
cars and hustling across intersections. I
move fast so I can set the box down sooner.
I stumbled into the Wythe Hotel, sweating
like a lunatic and scaring the Europeans.
But the hotel manager pays up front and puts
a copy in every room so it's always worth
the trouble. And between you and me, their
bar is a very nice place to have a drink.

DAY 29 - Tuesday, June 24 - [2:50am]

I have so much energy lately. Sometimes I
just break into a run for no reason. Like
when I am in the subway and there are stairs
I run up the stairs, for no reason - even
when I have dress shoes on. Sometimes I
wish it was okay for people to dance on
the street and in the subway because I was
listening to music on my headphones and I
felt like dancing. I felt like jumping
on park benches and throwing my shoulders
around. I felt like lip syncing to strange
girls and asking them to join me. I would

feel much better if we lived in a society
that accepted spontaneous dancing and
excessive drinking.

DAY 30 - Wednesday, June 25 - [1:22pm]

Eileen, I really don't like doing speaking
events. I turned down another speaking
event this morning. I don't like the idea
of talking about myself or being observed.
Too much attention is a bad thing. That's
why most bands who get a ton of press and
attention for their first album, put out
a shitty second album. There are too many
people watching. The things that happen
when no one is paying attention is something
that can't be recreated. If you look
directly at it, the thing will vanish.

DAY 30 - Wednesday, June 25 - [6:05pm]

I just got a call about Jake. He's having
some more trouble. I may have to go back
soon.

DAY 31 - Thursday, June 26 - [3:33am]

Eileen, I don't watch a lot of scary or
disturbing things. The other day, I saw
a movie poster in the subway. And at the

bottom it said, "Rated R for disturbing violence." I don't understand why people would want to watch something with disturbing violence. I'm very careful about what I put into my mind. I used to think that the way to really live life was to try and experience everything, even horrible and self-destructive things. I thought that happy people didn't really understand life and only tortured artists and people brave enough to go to dark places knew what life was really about. But the truth is, there is no bottom to darkness. You can go miles and miles into self-destructive and negative places until you're dead or do some truly horrible, irreversible damage. There is nothing to be learned in that head space. It is a fool's errand to try and force struggle or adversity. I'm not saying we should avoid painful situations just because they're difficult. I'm just saying it's best for everyone to stay out of trouble. And for me, I try to watch movies and TV shows that don't invoke anxiety or troubling thoughts.

DAY 32 - Friday, June 27 - [3:54am]

Woah. I had an intense dream. I was in the back of a pick-up truck with Kurt Cobain. He was still alive. He never died. He just quit the band. And he had been living

alone for many years. But he was making
a comeback. And I was there to help with
the day's events — assist him from the
rehearsal space to the hotel and then to the
venue the next day. But we had an intense
conversation in the back of that truck
about music and how he saw the world and I
remember thinking that his knowledge about
the music industry seemed grossly outdated.

DAY 33 - Saturday, June 28 - [4:28am]

Hi Eileen,
Tonight I wrote a story where the narrator
goes on a blind date but the date turns into
a very long and crazy night of drinking
together. First they start with a stroll
through Prospect Park. And they realize
that they really like each other. They
go to a liquor store and get a bottle of
booze. And the date turns into an 8 hour
adventure with packed lunches and bathroom
breaks in the bushes. And they get into a
little trouble with petty theft and climbing
on waterfalls and getting kicked out of the
park after sundown.

DAY 34 - Sunday, June 29 - [12:32am]

I had to go to St. Mark's bookshop today.
They keep asking me to do a reading. I had

to explain why I don't do them - people just
sit there in folding chairs and stare at
you. And you're supposed to pretend that
you're happy to be there. And although I
am thankful and humbled to be asked in the
first place, nothing makes me cringe more
than the idea of reading something I wrote
in front of other people.

I don't have much to say. I always picture
myself out in the audience rolling my eyes
at myself. "Get off your high horse you
dumb prick," I'd yell to myself. Maybe
that's not the best approach. It's a
terrifying thing – to take the 4AM drunken
confessions and read them in the daylight
in a room full of strangers. The worst that
could happen is that they could hang me
alive or I could self-induce a panic attack
that might trigger a real heart attack that
would result in my death before I was even
able to finish my second novel.

"He may have been a decent writer," they'll
say. "But he scared himself to death in
front of 17 people at a book reading."

DAY 35 - Monday, June 30 - [4:09am]

I really need to take a trip soon. I feel
like if I don't get out of here for a while,
I'm gonna lose it. Eileen, last summer, for

four days in a row, I had this dream that
someone said, "You have cancer," or "Someone
very close to you has cancer." It was a
dream so the words and faces were vague but
there was no doubt that either I had cancer
or someone very close to me did. I walked
around for months wondering what the hell
that dream meant until eventually I found
out about Jake. He was diagnosed with
melanoma this spring. Sometimes I wonder
if that dream was supposed to be some kind
of warning. But what was I supposed to do
about it? I couldn't ask everyone I knew to
get tested for cancer. The dream was just
too vague to be helpful.

DAY 36 - Tuesday, July 1 - [12:55am]

My friends and I have decided to drive up to
Providence, Rhode Island this weekend. I've
never been there before but I guess it's as
good a place as any. The important thing
is just to stop working for a couple days
and relax. Maybe I'll do whatever people
in Rhode Island do. Like take slow walks
and stir handcrafted fudge. But other than
that, it's just me and the bed and the room
service menu and maybe a couple of strolls
down main street. My friends booked the
hotel. It's called The Biltmore Hotel. I
looked it up online today and it turns out
there are all these blog posts and reviews

online about how the place is haunted. It
was supposedly founded by a Satanist who
originally built a chicken coop on the
roof to supply chickens for weekly Satanic
sacrifices. There's been reports of rape
and murder and at least 6 people have gone
missing. One of the Yelp reviewers said
that a ghost appeared in front of her bed
in the middle of the night and pulled the
sheets off the bed. Eileen, it doesn't
sound like a very relaxing place to stay.

DAY 37 - Wednesday, July 2 - [2:51am]

Eileen, I don't believe in ghosts. The idea
that you appear as a see-through body that
still wears clothes seems ridiculous. Why
do they have to wear the same clothes and
always look the same? Even the idea of a
stagnant soul seems ridiculous. We are
always changing. I am completely different
than I was when I was 6 years old. I bet
that happens after death too. Maybe your
spirit is pretty similar right after death
to what it was when you were alive. But
it keeps growing and changing. I bet it
evolves and eventually it becomes something
we can't even comprehend.

DAY 38 - Thursday, July 3 - [4:15am]

I'm not sure about this trip. Someone just told me that there is a hurricane coming up the East Coast. CNN says, "It's expected to bring storm surges of up to 5 feet, as well as large, damaging waves, high winds and dangerous rip currents that could sweep even the strongest swimmers out to sea." This is going to be the worst relaxing weekend ever.

I can't believe we're taking this road trip on the Fourth of July even though the fireworks are on the Brooklyn side this year. Are you going to watch the fireworks? If so, I hope you have a nice time and I hope they aren't cancelled because of the hurricane. Thanks for liking my Instagram picture today. I posted an excerpt from my new book and put up the pre-order link. I sold a lot of pre-orders in the last 12 hours. You left a comment on my post and said you really liked it. That made my day.

DAY 39 - Friday, July 4 - [12:29am]

Hi Eileen,
Almost every flight out of LaGuardia was cancelled yesterday. There was a line of 120 people at the car rental place. They wouldn't let us wait inside even though

we paid for our rental car in advance. My
friends and I were standing outside in
the rain when the storm turned dangerous.
The black clouds moved in. The wind and
lightning picked up.

The sky turned darker than I had ever seen
it before. Rain poured down and the wind
tossed umbrellas and suitcases around in the
parking lot until people began to push their
way inside. It was a complete disaster.
Sad souls were wringing out their clothes
in the bathroom and charging their phones in
the hallway. They were ordering pizzas and
sharing fighting with strangers. One lady
was yelling into her cell phone, "I don't
care if the delivery guy was just here. I'm
placing an order! This is a new order." We
saw that pizza guy show up three different
times before we finally got a car.

After driving and driving in the rain, we
finally arrived at our hotel in Providence.
My room doesn't seem to be haunted. But
they do not have a mini bar so we may go
out for drinks. It has been raining all day
and the fireworks have been postponed until
tomorrow. There are females friends who
came along on this trip. So I may see if
one of them would like to stay in my room.

DAY 40 - Saturday, July 5 - [4:24am]

Hi Eileen. Today was a much better day.
The rain stopped and my friends and I walked
around Providence. We saw many historical
things. We also went to the Rhode Island
School of Design Museum. They had magazines
and book covers and silkscreened posters.
It was great. And they had old school, punk
rock zines behind glass cases.

After that, we ate sushi and went on a
boat ride. Then later, we went to a
bookstore called "Symposium Books." I think
Providence is a pretty cool place after all.

DAY 41 - Sunday, July 6 - [4:36am]

Tonight in the hotel, I had a dream that
I was walking down Houston on my way back
to the subway. It was a beautiful summer
night and my buddy Jake was right there with
me. He was walking with me and I had my arm
around him because he was having trouble
walking. I'm not sure if it was because he
was drunk or sick but he needed somebody
to lean on. But other than a little
trouble walking, he seemed to be okay. He
was smiling. And the breeze smelled like
freshly cut grass. And I walked my friend
all the way home.

DAY 42 - Monday, July 7 - [12:18am]

We had to check out of the hotel at noon
and then we drove all the way back to
Brooklyn without stopping. I did most of
the driving. Everyone else was hungover.
I'm home now having a couple of drinks and
responding to messages on Instagram.

DAY 43 - Tuesday, July 8 - [2:46am]

Hi Eileen,
Last night I drank too much and sent you
a message on Instagram. I totally forgot
I did this until right before you replied.
I asked if I could send you a couple of
books. And you said sure and gave me your
address. That was a very strange feeling.
I was sitting here and I got this feeling –
a feeling that you were reading my message.
And you wrote me back about 30 seconds after
that feeling. The same thing happened to
me while I was trying to catch an M train
today. I was walking down the stairs and
there was a train sitting there. And I was
really surprised to see a train because my
gut was telling me I'd have to wait a while.
So I didn't run for it. The train doors
closed and it started to leave. But when I
got down there, I could see it wasn't even
my train. Does that ever happen to you? Do

you ever know you're going to get a phone
call right before it rings?

DAY 44 - Wednesday, July 9 - [12:13am]

Eileen, today I watched a documentary about
J.D. Salinger. He never spoke in public and
never did interviews. I think a good writer
needs to be able to see several different
viewpoints at once. And I think developing
a public persona can hinder this ability.
It's almost like playing a character when
you speak in front of a group. Even when I
write to you, I think about the "narrator."
Who is the narrator? Even though this is
my real life, there are many sides to the
same story. And it's my job to decide which
story to tell. So a real-life account of
my life could take the form of a thousand
different versions. We are all experiencing
many different and conflicting feelings
all at the same time. And when we speak
out loud or present ourselves to a group we
can only choose one of these people and the
others collapse into nothingness. Our true
self is really a collection of limitless
possibilities.

DAY 45 - Thursday, July 10 - [11:06pm]

Hey Eileen,
The sunset over Manhattan tonight was
extraordinary. The sky was all lit up with
a giant band of pink. And then it slowly
morphed into a deep purple color that rolled
over the whole skyline. And parts of the
sky shot off into streaks of blue and looked
like someone rubbed it up and down with an
eraser. I was cooking dinner and looking
at all the pictures on Instagram of the sky
tonight. It was cool to know that so many
people were looking at the same thing. I
even got a text that said, "Look at the
sky!"

It all made me feel like I was part of a
community. And that's what keeps us making
art I guess. Sometimes you don't have to
even meet in person to feel like you're
part of a community. As long as you're
expressing yourself and people are paying
attention, then you're connected to other
human beings. It's a very important part of
living a happy and meaningful life. Maybe
that's why you became an actress. Eileen,
I think if you find something you love and
you're good at it, you should find a way to
do that for the rest of your life. That's
not a selfish thing. Our art is always
presented to our community. This is why I

loved the sunset and Brooklyn today. This
is why I'm writing to you.

DAY 46 - Friday, July 11 - [4:47pm]

Eileen! Oh my God! Today on Instagram you
were soaring on the ropes doing the splits
and reaching out your arms like an eagle!
How do you stay on the bar without falling
to your death?! You are really something
else!

Who's Violet? Your caption said, "Violet
would have loved this."

DAY 46 - Friday, July 11 - [3:12am]

Today I was thinking about you because there
was a production company shooting a movie or
a TV show on my block. I was walking down
the street to the subway and a beautiful
actress walked out of her trailer and
looked me in the eye. She was an exquisite
sample of the human species. I'm not sure
what movie or TV show they were shooting
but people are always shooting stuff on my
block. There are a lot of film crews here.

Anyway, I was eye to eye with this beautiful
girl and I was wondering what her life was

like. Being a famous movie star isn't
what it used to be. Directors can buy nice
cameras for cheap. There aren't many people
getting rich from movies anymore but maybe
that's okay. Maybe that beautiful girl
coming out of her silver metal trailer won't
be able to buy a house in Malibu. But she
was on the goddamn television. And that's
something her grandmother can see and be
proud of.

Eileen, I can tell from your photos and
your video posts that you're lovely and
talented. And I hope you stay persistent
and optimistic long enough to get your shot
in this world. Maybe you won't have a ten
thousand dollar dress to show off at the
Grammys but I bet you'll be able to pay your
rent in royalty checks if you keep trying.

DAY 47 - Saturday, July 12 - [3:28am]

Eileen, today was rough. I was not feeling
well. I got stuck eating fish and chips
alone in a bar between soundcheck and set
time. And some Asian man at the bar was
hitting on me and I could have sworn he
was gay until he started showing me photos
on his phone of women's asses that he took
while walking behind them on the street.
And I could barely finish my food I was so
sick. That was the first show. Then I had

to carry 60 pounds of LPs by myself back to
my apartment and go to a second show. I
waited all the way until 2am. All I wanted
to do was say hello to the band and then
go home. And when I finally found the lead
singer, he looked at me and said, "Don't
talk to me right now, I'm in the middle of
something important." I wanted to hit him.
And then at 2:11AM, I got the call that Jake
died. I just sat in the street and cried.
Eventually I got in a cab and went home.

DAY 48 - Sunday, July 13 - [4:13am]

I didn't work today. I booked my flight and
also called Jake's family to tell them how
sorry I was. My father said he would pick
me up from the airport.

DAY 49 - Monday, July 14 - [9:47pm]

Hey Eileen,
I didn't get out of bed today until 1:30PM.
I made lunch and rented a movie. I had
about 200 emails but I just turned off my
phone and stayed on my couch. Then I took
a bath. I disconnected my computer and my
phone from the internet. I ate some dinner.
It's only 9:47PM and I'm about to go to
sleep.

DAY 50 - Tuesday, July 15 - [12:16am]

Hey Eileen,
Today, I stopped at this park in my
neighborhood that has a fountain and some
benches. There was no one there. It was
warm outside. It must have been 73 degrees
Fahrenheit – the ideal temperature. I laid
down on this bench and looked up at the
trees and thought about nothing. For a
second or two, I forgot I was in the city
and got lost in the breeze and the sunlight
shining through these giant branches gently
swaying under the sky.

I fly back to the Midwest tomorrow. They
asked me to speak at Jake's visitation.

DAY 51 - Wednesday, July 16 - [4:17am]

Eileen, I am in a hotel room in the Midwest
again. Goddamn this place. It's very
difficult here. The lights are dim. The
walls are dirty. I do not like coming here.
I would rather sleep outside on the ground
than in this awful fucking place.

DAY 52 - Thursday, July 17 - [12:40am]

I was so exhausted when I arrived at the
hotel yesterday that I collapsed on the bed

with my jeans on. I woke up at 6AM because
I forgot to close the curtains. I took a
bath and sat in there for a long time. This
room is so dingy. They don't have wifi and
there is no room service. I was afraid to
walk on the carpet with my bare feet after
I got out of the bath. I went outside and
took a long walk until I found a place that
had omelets.

I don't remember most of the day.

I said some things at Jake's visitation
service. But I don't remember what I said.
I think I was too sad to be nervous about
speaking. Also, writers aren't supposed
to say, 'sad.' We are supposed to say
something more original like, 'I felt like
walking into traffic and letting one of the
cars hit me.' That's what I meant by 'sad.'

Now that Jake is gone, it's become apparent
that I'm not much help to anyone here. His
parents and siblings are taking care of each
other, going through his clothes, sharing
photos, etc. I'm sort of the awkward friend
who doesn't quite fit in with the family. I
moved my flight a day earlier so I can leave
in the morning.

DAY 53 - Friday, July 18 - [3:19am]

Hi Eileen,
I'm back in New York today. It's pouring
rain tonight. I made salmon and sautéed
potatoes. I don't have to work tomorrow.
If I had my way, I'd be hunkered down with
a typewriter on a beach or in a secluded
cabin. I don't know why I don't go and do
something like that. I should go to Puerto
Rico. I'm not sure what's keeping me here.
The price of alcohol in Brooklyn is grossly
overpriced compared to the rest of the
country.

DAY 54 - Saturday, July 19 - [3:29am]

I don't feel like doing anything Eileen. I
should be promoting my books but I really
do not like promoting things. Eileen, when
you finish a project, do you enjoy all of
the promotional stuff? Or are you like a
shark who always keeps moving and never
reads press reviews? I'd rather be doing
something else. Maybe I could start a new
poetry book and dedicate it to Jake.

DAY 55 - Sunday, July 20 - [3:56am]

I was sitting on the East River. I saw a
young tree swaying on the water's edge. It

was a cotton tree. I recognized the leaves.
We used to have one in my family's front
yard growing up. I wondered how the hell it
got here on this meticulously landscaped New
York City park. There are no cotton trees
around here. The thing looked miserable
blowing around in the wind. It was not a
peaceful place for a young tree. I wondered
what was the point of it all? Why did that
tree want to grow so bad? And what about
all the other seeds that didn't make it? My
dad used to suck them up in the lawn mower.

I sat there for a while looking at this
little tree - blowing back and forth on the
edge of the river. Then something occurred
to me. Maybe we're incomplete without other
people to love. If we're all connected then
maybe that explained the beauty in sacrifice
and the importance of community. Maybe
that's why it was okay for a lion to eat
a deer. It was all one life force. But
still, when part of our life force didn't
make it, the rest of us felt sad. But maybe
the little cotton tree had a reason to hold
on in the wind. Maybe the earth just works
as one unit. We're all just different
expressions of the same force - like rolling
waves of energy. Maybe separateness is an
illusion. When someone dies, it's a part of
ourselves. We are all an ocean of energy.

DAY 56 - Monday, July 21 - [12:58am]

Dear Eileen,
Today was tricky. The problem was that
the wine store in my neighborhood closes
before I would be able to get a bottle of
wine. And I had to be in Times Square for
a meeting. And the gym I belong to has a
location with a pool so I decided to go
for a swim since I'd be close by. And it
started pouring rain. But I didn't care
because I knew I was going swimming anyway.
So I let it pour down on me.

I finally got to the gym and walked into
the locker room soaking wet. And all these
jock gym guys looked at me like I came from
another planet. I guess I should mention
that I have punk rock hair and all these
tattoos. And today, on top of my normal
appearance I was also completely soaking
wet. And I'm thinking, "Yeah, I know, I
don't fit in here but I'm just trying to use
the pool." So I stumble into that locker
room and as I was pulling out my swim trunks
my bottle of cabernet sauvignon flew out and
shattered on the floor. And all these jock
dudes just stared at me like I was some sort
of lunatic. They must have thought I was
mad using the white gym towels to clean up
all the broken glass and red wine. But all
I could think about was that I didn't have
anything left to drink.

DAY 57 - Tuesday, July 22 - [1:50am]

Today I am feeling better. I think I had a
little breakdown yesterday with that wine.
But I am feeling better today. I got two
interesting emails this afternoon. One was
from a Fortune 500 company asking me if I'd
come speak at their offices in Manhattan.
The other was from a 17 year old girl whose
parents wanted her to be a doctor or lawyer
but who said I had inspired her to become
a writer. I deleted the email from the
corporation and took an hour and a half to
write the girl back.

Eileen, do you know what I told that 17
year old girl about writing? I told her
to use a typewriter and don't publish
anything. Typewriters are great because
they enable a person to write things in a
bubble. There is no way to edit. There is
no way to copy and paste the words onto a
blog or an embarrassing Twitter post. It's
just the writer and the craft. And I told
her, as soon as you have a stack of pages
finished, the next thing you've got to do
is burn them. Don't send them to anyone
and don't publish them, just get rid of
them. Anything you write for the first 5 to
10 years will be embarrassing. Don't make
mistakes in the public eye. Keep it all
private until you hone your craft. And then
one day, you'll be reading some popular book

---

or website and you'll think to yourself,
"My stuff is better than this." That's when
it's time to publish.

DAY 58 - Wednesday, July 23 - [12:28am]

Eileen, I had another psychic thing happen
to me today. I was working at home and I
got this strong sense that my friend Patti
was thinking about me. It was an intense,
strong feeling. I knew that she was
thinking about me (the good and the bad).
And it felt VERY real. This is someone I
have never even met in person but we used
to email back and forth almost every week
while she was helping me with a project
last year. But I have not heard from her
in MONTHS. So there I was with this very
strong feeling. And I was looking on my
phone and constantly refreshing my email
to see if she wrote me. And I was checking
Twitter. And I even say out loud, "Why do
I have this intense feeling that Patti is
thinking about me right now?" And about 15
seconds later she Tweets me. She replied to
some ancient Tweet from last year and said,
"Just catching up on Twitter. I hope your
summer is going well."

Somebody told me once that you can tell if
you're having an intuitive experience if the
thought appears out of nowhere. If you can

48

follow your train of thoughts and logically
follow where the thought came from, it's
normal brain activity. But if the feeling
or thought seems to pop up with no trigger
or explanation, it could be information
being transmitted from somewhere else. This
is what keeps happening to me.

DAY 58 - Wednesday, July 23 - [12:53am]

Also, Eileen, I forgot to tell you, the
other day I was on my way to the Bowery and
accidentally walked down the wrong street
and there was some theatre performance in
a parking lot. I think they were doing a
Shakespeare play. They had plastic chairs
set up in a circle. There must have been
200 people there - silently watching in
this parking lot. The acting was exquisite
and the performance was beautiful. And I
thought about you and this city of ours. I
thought about how lucky we are to live here.
Things are so competitive that you really
need to be special in order to survive in
New York. But the great thing is that there
is inspiration everywhere. We cannot walk
through a subway without hearing some of the
most talented musicians in the world. We
cannot take a wrong turn through a parking
lot without seeing Shakespeare.

DAY 59 - Thursday, July 24 - [4:12am]

Dear Eileen,
Today I went over to a new bookstore because
they emailed me about wanting to carry my
stuff. It was nice. I met the owner and
she had a very kind soul. She even gave me
a tiny bundle of sage. She told me how to
use it around my apartment. We talked for
a while about book distribution and what it
was like owning a business. I really liked
her. She said she and her husband sometimes
have bar-b-ques in the back of their store
and I should come to the next one.

After that, I had to go to Spoonbill and
Sugartown to pick up some money. They sold
out of my book in 4 days. I don't even have
any more. I ordered some but they won't be
here until next week.

Then I had a meeting with a band manager who
represents a very large rock band. I won't
say which one but they were inducted into
the Rock & Roll Hall of Fame recently and
have sold over 9 million records. He said
he's been reading my books and really liked
them and thought it would be nice to meet
up since we both live in New York. He was
a really good guy. We got along right away.
He asked me if I'd ever consider writing
a biography about a famous band and I said

probably not. He asked me why but I really
didn't have an answer. So I told him I'd
think about it some more and let him know.

After saying goodbye and heading for the
train, I walked past McCarren Park I noticed
a band playing and a crowd of people
dancing. It was Janelle Monae shooting a
Pepsi commercial. She was really working
the crowd. I stopped and watched for a
while. She was very good. It was only
about 50 people dancing and clapping and
singing along. The drummer was just some
guy banging away on upside-down buckets.
And Janelle was really hamming it up for
the cameras and dancing and playing with
the crowd. I met her once in Chicago. I
would have said hi but she was pretty busy
getting all those people riled up for the
commercial. I felt at peace and happy to be
in Brooklyn.

DAY 60 - Friday, July 25 - [1:53am]

Eileen, after that meeting yesterday,
I realized that I have no idea how to
write a book about a rock band. I'm not
a journalist. The only way I would know
how to do it is just to ride along on the
tour bus and tell the story exactly as it
happened. And if the band was boring I
would have to do things like start fights

and hook up with their girlfriends just so I
would have something to write about.

But then I had so many questions like, who
would own the book? Who would pay for
my food? Would I have to pay the band
royalties every time I sold a book? And
so on. I am really not experienced in the
publishing industry. So I emailed this guy
I thought would know, Michael Azerrad. He
wrote a popular book about Nirvana and a
couple others.

He said that as long as I didn't sign a
contract with the band for an "Authorized"
book, I would retain the rights and wouldn't
need to pay anyone royalties. It would
be a work of journalism told from my
experience. He said: "When I spoke with
Kurt Cobain about the possibility of writing
a biography of Nirvana, I said, "This won't
be an authorized biography, right?" And
Kurt said, "Oh no, that would be too Guns
'n' Roses." Kurt trusted me to write an
accurate book. That's what you want with
your project."

Thank goodness for Kurt Cobain and Michael
Azerrad.

DAY 61 - Saturday, July 26 - [1:50am]

Hi Eileen,
A good friend of mine had a show at Cake
Shop tonight. The last time I was there was
with Jake, actually. I was still living in
the Midwest. But the two of us had come
to town for a music festival. And it was
after 2am at a Vice after party. There were
women falling out of their clothes and a
large crowd of people doing cocaine in the
bathroom. This was several years ago. And
I remember thinking that we were all going
to be trapped in that basement. The floor
has a very steep slope downwards towards the
back of the basement.

And I was so fucked up. I think I had taken
drugs or something. And I thought for
sure if one person fell over, every person
in the room would tumble on those slanted
floors and no one would be able to get back
up. The crowd would collapse, the band
would collapse, the drums would collapse
and we'd all go sliding into that corner.
And it would be impossible to get back up
again. It was like some weird funhouse
and someone decided to start selling booze
and demanded that bands play right there
on these terrible slanted floors. And I
never went back to the Cake Shop because
as far as I was concerned we were all on
drugs and we were all going to die or get

sucked into that corner and never get up
again. But tonight I had to go back and it
wasn't so bad. I wondered what Jake would
have thought of the place if he could see it
again. The worst part about the show was
that the bar gin did not taste right and
their tonic was flat. Jake always liked
tequila though.

DAY 61 - Saturday, July 26 - [2:17am]

Also, I decided I'm not going to write that
rock band biography. There are a lot of
journalists out there that can do that sort
of thing. I'm going to keep going with what
I do.

DAY 62 - Sunday, July 27 - [2:09am]

Eileen, sometimes I look at your Instagram
photos and I think this book of mine is a
really stupid idea. I mean, technically we
don't even know each other. I thought this
was interesting when I first started. Maybe
it was even an indirect commentary on the
modern era. But lately I've been thinking
it's just weird and unnatural. Maybe that's
a side-effect of these new technologies. We
just watch each other from a distance and
feel lonely. We try to impress each other.

But our lives are never as clever as our posts online.

DAY 63 - Monday, July 28 - [2:16am]

I woke up in the morning, made breakfast and lit the sage that my new friend gave me. I walked around the apartment with that sage. I know it's probably stupid but I felt better after I did it. I think just the act of doing something like that is where the real secret lies. Our minds are immensely powerful. Sometimes believing is enough. It's like if you tell someone, "If you stand on one foot for seven days, you will find your soulmate on the 8th day." And the person stands there with their damn foot in the air. And nothing is really happening except in that person's mind. So on the 8th day, they go out in the world and they see a person they are attracted to and their confidence is so overwhelmingly high that they find their motherfucking soulmate.

It's all about the mind, really. I'm not into new age spiritual stuff. But I am a firm believer that reality is an elastic thing. I think that we have an ability to use our imagination and CHOOSE to view the world in the way we want it to be. I think the outside world molds and fits into our

viewpoint and we can have a strong impact on
our surroundings.

DAY 63 - Monday, July 28 - [3:47am]

Eileen, who is Violet? You posted a photo
today that said, "Violet the unstoppable."
And it was a photo of you and a beautiful
blonde girl standing by the river in
Brooklyn Bridge Park. But you looked
different. You looked younger and your hair
was a different color. Even your eyebrows
were a slightly different shape. Did you
lose your friend, Violet? You didn't tag
anyone. Where is Violet now?

DAY 64 - Tuesday, July 29 - [3:28am]

Hey Eileen,
My friend's band played at Rough Trade
tonight. We all went to dinner afterward
and saw Mike O'Brien from Saturday Night
Live on the street. Then we went to this
restaurant on Bedford called Allswell. I
was talking to this long-haired bearded man
for about an hour. And he was telling me
about how he was on a diet where the only
thing he was allowed to eat was meat and
vodka. I really liked him. We decided to
keep in touch so he gave me his phone and
email. And when he told me his name, I

realized he was a famous producer and made
albums for Aerosmith, Twisted Sister, Bruce
Springsteen, Dinosaur Jr., Jawbox, Patti
Smith, Sonic Youth and Social Distortion.

I couldn't believe I was talking to this
famous music producer and didn't even
realize it. It's nice to be reminded about
how we all live in a small world. And we
don't even need to try too hard. We can
just show up and be nice to people and work
on really cool things together. I think
that's something important to remember.
Just show up and be nice to people.

DAY 65 - Wednesday, July 30 - [2:50am]

Hey Eileen,
Urban Outfitters emailed me today. They
said they were considering carrying my
poetry book in their stores. Can you
believe it? The buyer said she had
a meeting next week and asked me some
questions about wholesale pricing. I sent
her the info and now I just have to wait
to find out if they want it or not. I try
not to get too excited until things are
confirmed. And even if they actually take
the books, I'm not sure that people who shop
at Urban Outfitters actually read.

DAY 66 - Thursday, July 31 - [12:01am]

Today you posted a photo of yourself wearing
a designer T-shirt. The shirt said, "These
Are The Days" and you linked to the designer
in your comments. I think this is a good
sign, Eileen. I think this means you are
making money with your skills. At the very
least, I hope you are getting some free
clothes in exchange for posting pictures
like that. I hope you're out there making
dreams happen, Eileen.

DAY 67 - Friday, August 1 - [3:57am]

A friend of mine debuted a film tonight
at Nitehawk Cinema. I got there late and
couldn't find a seat. I didn't eat anything
before I got there because they serve food.
But the waitresses wouldn't serve me dinner
unless I was in a seat. So all I could do
was have drinks on an empty stomach and
try not to stumble over as the waitresses
came breezing in and out of the theatre
with trays of food. I don't remember what
the movie was about. It was some sort of
documentary. I just kept ordering drinks
and tried to stay out of the way.

Eileen, I miss Jake. I don't like being
home alone right now. I am on the internet
looking for events to go to tomorrow.

DAY 68 - Saturday, August 2 - [2:52am]

Tonight I went to the Museum of Art and
Design to see a film about Kurt Cobain
and Nirvana. The film was shit. It was
basically just a collection of YouTube
videos and other documentaries stitched
together in chronological order. But it was
nice to be in a room full of people who like
Nirvana as much as I do.

After the movie, I went for a walk in
Central Park. I strolled east and passed
the pond. I climbed up the big boulders of
schist rock that overlook the city and the
ice rink. Eileen, I think that might be one
of my favorite spots in all of New York.
And I love New York so that makes it one of
my favorite spots on planet earth and by
default, the universe. Those rocks and the
skyline south of 59th street have got to be
one of the most beautiful views in the city.

I sat there for a long time and thought
about Jake. One of the last times I saw
him I told him I was thinking about going to
Puerto Rico and swimming with sea turtles.
Maybe I should go there soon.

I sat on those rocks and tried to give
myself a break from all my thoughts and
worries. I tried to let it all go. But
there were too many people around, making

noise. And the mosquitos kept biting my
arms so I l headed home.

On my way out, I noticed that all the dirt
in Central Park is packed down hard with the
millions of footprints of everyone who's
ever stepped there. And it made me realize
that more people have stepped on one square
inch of that dirt than I have ever met in
my life. I started to wonder about all the
people I have actually met. Like how many
people have I actually introduced myself to
and learned something about them? I don't
think it's very many.

DAY 69 - Sunday, August 3 - [3:30am]

Eileen, when I was a kid I watched this guy
on TV who won a chance to win a million
dollars during half-time at a big football
game.

All he had to do was throw a football
across the field and through a rubber
tire. But the tire was very far away. Even
professional football players couldn't do
it. The TV people interviewed him at half-
time and he said he was a pastor at his
church and he was going to win the million
dollars and donate it to his congregation.
Even as a kid watching on TV, I remember
thinking that he seemed so sure of himself.

Eileen, do you know what happened? He
tossed that football all the way across that
field. It sailed through the air, sloped
down in a perfect arch and went straight
through that little rubber tire.

I think faith is important - not in some
bearded man in the sky but in something
outside ourselves. I think faith is what
carries us and drags us out of negative
places. It enables us to accomplish things
that would normally be impossible. I bet
it even changes our brain chemistry and our
skill level. It's like a secret type of
magic that beats science every time.

So if you find yourself down or being
rejected at too many auditions, just
remember to keep your strength where no
one can get to it. Keep your faith in a
place that isn't affected by online reviews
or social status. It could be love for
somebody. It could be honoring someone's
memory or even that feeling of flow that
we get from our work - that connection to
something greater. Guard it, Eileen. Keep
your strength in a place where trolls can't
fuck with it.

DAY 70 - Monday, August 4 - [2:49am]

Eileen, I have been laying around the
apartment for too many hours in a row.
I've been editing new poetry but all the
words are blurring together. Supposedly
the sun came up and set and it was a very
nice day. I have no idea what happened out
there because I was too busy working. And
I was changing little things like compliment
to complement and looking up to see if
fingernails was indeed one word. This is
the worst part about being a writer. It's
like being trapped in a story. You can't
leave until every word is right. The city
looks and feels very overwhelming when you
go outside. The traffic lights move as you
walk and they don't do that in your stories.

DAY 71 - Tuesday, August 5 - [1:26am]

Hey Eileen,
Tonight my buddy invited me out to watch The
Karate Kid at Bryant Park. I'm glad he did.
I couldn't handle any more editing. The
final edits are always the hardest. It's
like when you know you and your girlfriend
are broken up for good but you still have
to be cordial and help her pack her shit and
carry boxes down to the moving truck to get
her out of your life forever. I'm tired of

the stuff I've been working on. I would
much rather just smoke cigarettes and be a
house painter or something. That seems much
more realistic than attempting to capture
something on a blank page.

It's days like these that I want to take up
something less subjective - like furniture
making. If you can sit in it, then it's a
chair.

DAY 72 - Wednesday, August 6 - [3:02am]

Hey Eileen,
I booked a flight to Puerto Rico! I am so
excited. I'm going to go see my old friend
Doug in San Juan and then I'm going to stay
on a beach in Culebra for 14 days. I am
going to sleep in a tent and go snorkeling
and swim with sea turtles. I haven't been
camping since I was 8 years old. My dad
took me once and it was horrible. We had
an old propane heater that my dad bought
at a garage sale. But the burner went out
half-way through the night and the fuel
kept leaking out. We all woke up freezing
and suffocating from the fumes. We had to
run out of there into the cold night and
the ground was frozen and I just wanted to
go home. But not this time, Eileen. This
time I'll have seafood and white sand and
thousands of neon fish. This time I'll

have beautiful people and I'll cook my own
food like a homeless man sleeping in the 5th
Avenue stop.

DAY 73 - Thursday, August 7 - [4:10am]

Today I did superyoga and meditated for an
hour. I'm trying to cut back on my drinking
and meditation helps with that. I need to
get my life back on track, Eileen. I can't
be feeling sorry for myself all of the time.
I miss my friend Jake. But I can be on
track and still miss my friend at the same
time.

Eileen, I hope you're out there hustling and
making calls. And I hope you're talking
yourself into being optimistic on the days
you feel like giving up. Because a smile
and the right set of eyes really opens more
doors than bitching about your day. Nobody
likes a complainer. So we do yoga or we go
to the gym for a swim and leave with a clear
mind. And when we get up the next morning
we feel stronger.

DAY 74 - Friday, August 8 - [3:16am]

Today I went to Generation Records and
dropped off some books. I walked through

Washington Square Park and went under the
arch just for the hell of it. I went down
to Other Music on 4th Street and I picked up
money for some books that sold. And then I
walked down to St. Mark's Books. They had
to move into a new location because they
were having trouble paying rent at the old
place. They're not sure how much longer
they'll be in business. But the new place
is pretty nice. It's much brighter and
fresher feeling. I picked up some money
from them too. And the guy there told me to
bring some more books when I have them.

DAY 75 - Saturday, August 9 - [1:56am]

I saw your tweet this morning and I hope
you had a great audition today. I'm not
sure what it was for but I hope you get the
part. Don't give up, Eileen. All of the
rejections and failures are just a temporary
thing. It's just the Universe testing your
optimist muscles.

Eileen, do you live paycheck to paycheck?
How are you able to audition and do readings
and all these time consuming things for
free? Do you work a waitress job or
something with flexible hours? I hope you
are out there hustling. I hope you don't
have rich parents or some sort of gifted
money. There's something about learning

and earning for yourself that makes success
taste a whole lot sweeter.

I know it's not always easy. The thing
about making art is that you are molding
entire worlds and battling all sorts of
giant enemies and problems. And you are
breaking the laws of physics and discovering
new planets and perfecting your skills and
getting lost in the flow. And when you
come out of it, the world has no idea what
happened. They don't know that you've just
been to outer space and flown around a black
hole and added decades of love and life and
experience to your soul. To them you look
just the same. And that thing you made,
that thing you dedicated your life to - they
call it a hobby. But it's still worth it,
Eileen. The alternative is very empty and
lonely.

We should do everything we can. Only time
will tell if we'll be good enough to catch
on. We just have to wait to see if our
little fire starts to spread. One can never
know for sure about these things. Sometimes
you can work for years and not even see
smoke.

DAY 76 - Sunday, August 10 - [2:30am]

Hello Eileen,
Tonight I spent a very long time marketing
my books. Also, all of the Rocky movies are
on Netflix right now. There is this one
scene in the first Rocky movie where Rocky
says to Adrian, "Can't do it." And she's
like, "What?" And Rocky says, "I can't beat
him. I been watchin' the moves, studying.
He ain't weak nowhere." And Rocky lays down
next to Adrian and says, "It don't matter
if I lose. The only thing that I wanna do
is go the distance. That's all. Nobody's
ever gone fifteen rounds with Creed. If I
go them fifteen rounds, and that bell rings
and I'm still standing, I'm gonna know
then I weren't just another bum from the
neighborhood."

I think that's what being an artist is
really about. We're not always going to
win. But if we can find a way to survive,
if we can figure out a way to structure our
lives so that we don't die or go bankrupt,
then we'll always be able to wake up the
next morning and continue to do what we
love. As long as we can do that, we'll be
okay.

DAY 777 - Monday, August 11 - [1:59am]

Eileen, I woke up hungover. I felt like an
idiot though because I realized that I got
so drunk I direct messaged Gerard Way from
My Chemical Romance on Twitter. I asked him
if he'd put me on the guestlist for his show
even though we've never actually met.

So I was really down on myself for drunk
messaging Gerard Way on Twitter. But then
a few hours later he messaged me back and
said, "Yes! Do you need a plus one?"

I guess sometimes we just need to be calm
and see the world as a kind place. And
realize that we are all just people. And
most of the people in this world are
generally nice and have good hearts and good
intentions.

Eileen, sometimes it's really important to
be ridiculous with what you think you can
accomplish and really push the limits.

When I was in college, I emailed the
president of the university and asked if I
could job shadow him for a day. We met very
early in the morning and he said that no one
had ever asked to job shadow him before. I
didn't even think about it. My professor
told us we needed to job shadow someone so

I emailed the most important person at the
university.

On the day I met with him, he scheduled an
hour that morning to talk with me and give
me some tips on how to be a president of a
university. He told me he started his day
by running 5 miles on his treadmill. Then
he ate a full breakfast with his wife. Then
he got to the office before anyone else and
did a couple of hours of work.

I followed him around for the whole day.
First he took a meeting about curriculum.
Then we walked over to the campus radio
station and he recorded an announcement
to promote an event on campus. He had a
wonderful speaking voice and a lot of public
speaking experience. He was on the debate
club and other speaking organizations when
he was younger. He did not seek out the
position of president. It was offered to
him unexpectedly.

People stopped him on the quad. He always
smiled and shook the students' hands. He
treated everyone with respect and always
seemed genuinely interested and never in
a rush. But he was extremely busy. His
calendar was packed with colorcoded meetings
and appointments.

Most people make little plans. They don't

go in a consistent direction. They get
burnt out. But successful people take
huge deliberate steps in a very focused
direction. They are Godsteppers. They
don't let fear stop them. They just go.
They know how to make things happen and
dedicate themselves to the cause.

The president's schedule was full with
football games, fundraisers and community
gatherings. He was even raising two
daughters and seemed to have a strong
relationship with his family. And the
thing I liked the most about him was that
when the two of us were talking, there was
no bullshit. He wasn't trying to sell me
anything or put on a show. I don't think he
even thought of our meeting as "student" and
"President." We just sat down like a couple
of human beings.

I think a secret to being successful is to
know that nothing is out of reach. All of
the actors with million dollar careers are
just people too. We don't need to separate
ourselves from anyone, Eileen. We can
work on ourselves and become good enough to
perform on the same level as these people.
We just have to work hard. But we can all
be Godsteppers - as long as we are brave
enough to look ourselves in the mirror and
grow in a way that enables us to take giant
steps forward.

DAY 78 - Tuesday, August 12 - [8:54pm]

Hey Eileen,
Today, a woman called me asking to be my
literary agent. But I don't want a literary
agent. I went to the flea market in Hell's
Kitchen and just wandered around and looked
at things. Then I went back to Brooklyn
and wandered over to McCarren park and sat
on a bench for a while. Some of the leaves
are starting to fall already. I feel like
I've been working so hard that I missed the
summer. I sat there for a long time. When
the wind blows across all that grass and you
can smell the trees, it can really bring
a person back - especially at this time
of year. I'm looking forward to spending
some time on a beach. I'm a little nervous
about Puerto Rico. I've never been camping
by myself before. I had to do a lot of
research online about camping supplies.

DAY 79 - Wednesday, August 13 - [12:35pm]

Eileen, I woke up from some fucked up
dreams this morning. I was so exhausted
last night that I fell asleep early. And
today I woke up at like 6am with all these
crazy, supernatural dreams. I had a dream
that I died. I couldn't fall back asleep
so I just got up. Eileen, do you think
your consciousness still exists after you

die? Even if it's just for a second, can
your consciousness exist without a body? I
have this coffee maker in my kitchen. It's
one of those Keurigs that has a little
'brew' light on the front. And the light
stays on for a split second after I unplug
it from the wall. Do you think life is
like that? Like if you had a little mouse
running around and you slammed down on it at
the speed of light, would it's consciousness
still be thinking, "Cheese, cheese, cheese?"

DAY 80 - Thursday, August 14 - [2:00am]

I meditated today. It's alarming how much
junk is floating around in my head: fears
and memories of things that never actually
happened. I worry about scenarios that
don't make sense. I get stuck on a thought
like a dog on a scent. My dumb bastard mind
just follows that scent trail right through
traffic without ever looking up. And the
dog gets so far away from home that he
forgets how to get back. And a rain comes
and the scent is gone and he's in a town
he's never been to before and forgets how
he got there in the first place. So I sit.
I sit and I watch these strange thoughts
come and go. Terrifying beasts walk past.
There's an 800 pound green lizard with a
club foot and fangs bigger than carrots.
And I look him in the eye because it's all

I can do. And eventually, after I sit
for enough time, he moves on with little
incident.

DAY 80 - Thursday, August 14 - [4:06am]

I think about Jake every day. His parents
didn't have the password to his Facebook
account. So he keeps popping up in my feed
whenever someone posts on his page. It's
so fucking sad. It is hard to care so much
about a person. Maybe this is why a lot
of people in New York are uncomfortable
in relationships. You start to become
entwined. You become one unit. And the
idea of existing outside of yourself can be
severely overwhelming.

DAY 81 - Friday, August 15 - [12:32am]

I went to Tent and Trails downtown and
bought a tent and big camping backpack.
And after that I went to the scuba store
and bought a snorkel, mask and fins. I
researched online about the island I'll be
staying at. There aren't many stores there.
I may need to bring some food with me. And
maybe one of those little gas stoves so I
can cook my food. I just realized, I leave
for Puerto Rico in 5 days. I am so excited.
Today was a good day.

DAY 81 - Friday, August 15 - [1:13am]

Eileen, there is this tree that I walk past
every time I go to do my laundry. And it
has all these old cobblestones stuck in
its trunk. They're embedded in the tree.
They're lifted right off the ground and just
stuck in there for good. I bet the tree can
feel them in there. It probably has no idea
what they are but the tree can feel them.
People have this type of thing too. We get
into emotional trouble or experience weird
energies that we can't explain. We just
feel it. Sometimes we're just growing into
a fence and have some chained link in our
trunk. Sometimes there's some cobble stones
in our way - a strange force that we can't
see but we can feel. Maybe it hurts but if
we're calm and determined, we'll find a way
to keep growing anyway. Eileen, sometimes
the wiser and more interesting trees are the
ones with metal sticking in them. They've
really been tested and they know themselves
a little better.

DAY 82 - Saturday, August 16 - [12:12am]

Eileen, I am really sorry about Violet.
Today you posted: "I miss you so much,
Violet. You continue to inspire even from
the heavens. I can't believe it's been
a year already. You used to say, "Tell me

the story of the sun and the moon." And I'm
just starting to understand. I think about
you every day, love."

I know we are strangers but I'm sorry,
Eileen. I'm sure your friend Violet was a
really beautiful person.

DAY 83 - Sunday, August 17 - [4:14am]

Eileen, I wish there was something I could
do. And maybe it's not my place to say but
I bet Violet loves you very much and is
really proud of you.

DAY 84 - Monday, August 18 - [12:30am]

Eileen, tonight I took the M train down
to Essex and walked over to St. Mark's
Bookshop. I walked around for a while with
my headphones on. It was such a beautiful
night. The smell of leaves in the air. I
really love New York at this time of year.
It must be the most beautiful place in the
world. The air was crisp and cool. And the
neon signs and the bars were all lit up.
And even the people on the street seemed
to be in a good mood. Maybe because the
weather is nice. Maybe because there are
always good things going on here.

Eileen, I just realized that we only have a couple more weeks left together. That was the idea wasn't it? 100 days of letters to my friend Eileen from Instagram? I hope I did okay.

People might not like this book but that's okay. A couple years from now, everyone will be using a different form of communication and this book will be outdated. That's okay, too. Everything becomes outdated eventually. Even our language will evolve and change. Slang words will turn into real words and all of my writing will eventually read like Olde English. It's just how the world works. Today we're sexy. Edgy. We own this fucking city. Tomorrow we're stuffy. Old-fashioned. Dust.

DAY 85 - Tuesday, August 19 - [2:11am]

Hey Eileen,
Today I went down to the Village (close to where you saw that Buddhist Monk). I had to go down to the record store and drop off some of my books. Then walked over to Washington Square Park and listened to a Spotify playlist on my phone. There were all sorts of people out. There were homeless men smoking pot and parts of

---

cigarettes that they picked up off the
street.

There were tourists wandering through the
arch and a girl that was crying so much that
her makeup was running down her cheeks. And
there is a guy down there who always feeds
the pigeons. He lets the dirty fucking
birds sit on his head and eat right out of
his hand. It's disgusting. No one sits
next to him because he is always covered in
shit.

I heard someone playing a piano so I walked
over towards 6th Ave. Some pianist had
dragged a full grand piano off of a truck
and wheeled it right into the park. He
wasn't a bad piano player. He wasn't the
best either. I listened to him play Chopin
and Rachmaninoff and Liszt and Brahms.
People were walking by and dropping dollar
bills into his bucket.

But then he played something really special.
He played Claude Debussy's "Clair De Lune."
Do you know this song? Eileen, I had mad
visions of Jake and his cancer was gone and
somehow he was okay. And I couldn't put it
into words but I had this intense feeling
that somehow I had to give this feeling to
you so that you knew about Violet. And I
had to keep it together on that park bench.
Because even if I couldn't give you that

feeling or explain the things without words,
I had to have faith that you would manage
without my help. And that seemed like a lot
to hope for.

But the leaves were changing and good things
always happened when the leaves change. I
was sitting in Washington Square Park where
the breeze was cool again. We would be
okay. I was in the place where Ginsberg
strolled and where Marcel Duchamp and
friends had a picnic on top of the arch and
refused to come down.

I had fought so hard over the years to be
able to sit on that bench. And in that
moment it felt so easy. It all felt so
easy. And maybe we can never let go of
the longing we have or the discomfort we
carry around with us. But sometimes, when
the breeze is just right and we can smell
freshly cut grass, it can feel like those
weights lift up for once. And we can
remember what it feels like for things to
be easy again. And if it ever seems too
hard to keep going, at the very least we can
get ahold of some grand piano and push the
fucking thing into the middle of Washington
Square Park and play out our troubles for
everyone else to hear.

DAY 86 - Wednesday, August 20 - [1:47am]

Eileen, I leave for Puerto Rico tomorrow and
I'm glad I'll be getting away for a while.
I'm excited to live on a beach with no
internet or phone reception. I just looked
at a calendar and counted the days that I've
been writing you. It looks like my last day
on the island will be on our 100th day. It
must be fate, Eileen. I have my bag all
packed and my boarding pass on my phone.
I've got an early flight and I'll write you
after I arrive.

DAY 86 - Wednesday, August 20 - [2:29am]

Eileen, I just want to thank you again for
following me on Instagram. It was nice to
have someone to write to while Jake was in
the hospital. So thanks for that. And
it was nice to live vicariously through
some sexy acrobat, strutting her stuff and
flexing her acting chops in the Brooklyn
theatre scene not too far from here. I
guess writing and acting aren't so different
after all. I needed a friend and there you
were swinging from a rope and liking my
posts. Thanks for keeping me company for a
while even though we've never met. Thanks
for being a friend even though it's a bit
unconventional.

DAY 87 - Thursday, August 21 - [4:44am]

Eileen,
Today was a cold morning in New York. I
took a cab to JFK with my giant backpack
and all my camping gear. I had my sleeping
bag and my snorkel gear and all the clothes
and supplies I needed for two weeks. And I
fell asleep on the plane. When I woke up,
I was in Puerto Rico. San Juan is a strange
place. It's nice and warm and you can feel
the ocean breeze no matter where you are.
But there are bars on most of the windows
here and a lot of abandoned buildings in
the city. Doug picked me up from the
airport and gave me a little tour around his
neighborhood. We walked around and looked
at some really great street art. Then we
went to the beach with his girlfriend Lisa
and had some drinks.

Doug pointed out all these sea turtle nests
on the beach. The city protects them with
orange plastic fencing. And when the sea
turtles hatch, giant crowds of people come
to watch. Doug said that the police come
with special red lights and everyone is very
quiet while the baby turtles crawl off into
the sea. I hope I am able to swim with some
turtles while snorkeling this week. I leave
for the campground in Culebra tomorrow. San
Juan is very nice but there are less people

in Culebra. It's a very small island and
it's quiet.

The three of us kept drinking on the beach
until we finished Doug's bottle of rum.
Then we went out to a restaurant for food
and more drinks. Somehow we ended up in
Santurce where Doug knew the owner of a
bar and they kept making us more drinks.
I think maybe we almost got into a fight
with somebody on the street. There were
thousands of people partying in the streets
of Santurce. The last thing I remember
we were at some karaoke bar and I was so
trashed that they kicked us out. Eileen, I
have been drinking a lot since Jake died.
I was drinking when he was diagnosed and I
was drinking when he was in the hospital.
And I drank even more when they stopped his
treatment and said the best thing to do was
just to make him comfortable. And I was
drinking every time I went to visit. And I
was drunk when he died. I think it's time
to stop, Eileen.

DAY 88 - Friday, August 22 - [4:08pm]

This morning was a little hectic. I
overslept and then had to run over to Doug's
apartment and wake him up. He drove me
across the island and dropped me off so that
I could catch the ferry to Culebra. It was

a big boat and took about an hour and a half
to get here.

Right now I am writing you from the
campground on Flamenco Beach. Eileen, this
island is not like the rest of the world. I
am on this beautiful beach and it feels like
I am living inside a postcard. I have my
tent set up right next to the ocean. The
water is so calm and clear, you can see all
the way to the bottom. There is a gentle
breeze that keeps the sand off my towel.
When I get too hot, I float in the turquoise
water or just walk out as far as I can
without having to swim. And then after a
while of being in the water, I come back to
my towel and lay in the sun and read or just
rest. Eileen, this is like heaven. It's
very peaceful. I'll post a picture on my
Instagram so you can see it.

There are chickens running around with
little baby chicks. And there are beautiful
people walking around half-naked. I jumped
in the water a little while ago with my
snorkel and saw a giant barracuda floating
right under the surface of the waves. The
water is very shallow for many yards out.
I'm just sitting here listening to the waves
and writing you. It's wonderful.

DAY 88 - Friday, August 22 - [10:45pm]

Eileen, it's the middle of the night. Some
creature was just outside my tent making a
lot of noise. I didn't know what it was. I
was shining my flashlight outside my tent.
I was even kicking the side of my tent to
try and scare it off. I was dumb enough to
keep food in my tent. I didn't think there
was anything big enough to bother me on the
island. But this thing sounded huge. My
imagination was getting the best of me. I
thought for sure it was some sort of giant
beast. It was going to bite chunks out of
my flesh while I was asleep. There are no
doctors on this island. I was going to
bleed out.

Something was definitely out there. And
earlier when I was outside brushing my teeth
in the dark, there were bats flying around
everywhere. They swooped down close to my
head because they were catching bugs. But
whatever was outside my tent was bigger
than a bat or anything that was known to
inhabit this island. Or so I thought. I
kept shining my flashlight outside to see if
I could spot something. And then finally,
I spotted it. About 8 feet from my tent,
rustling in the palm leaves, there it was -
a land crab. A little harmless land crab.
I even said out loud to myself, "A crab?
That's it?"

And now I'm going back to sleep, Eileen.
The waves are very loud outside my tent.
The tide comes in at night and the beach
shrinks and the waves are louder. I like it
very much, Eileen. It's very calming.

DAY 89 - Saturday, August 23 - [9:12pm]

I woke up this morning at 6AM because the
roosters were yelling. There was the most
beautiful sunrise coming up over the water
and lighting up the whole island with its
warm golden hue. And I stretched my arms
and legs and for once I felt well-rested. I
cracked open a coconut and drank the juice
for breakfast. It was just me and some
giant black and white crane sitting on the
beach watching the sunrise.

I needed some food and fuel for my stove
so I hitchhiked to the grocery store. I
researched all this online ahead of time and
knew exactly where to go. But Supermercado
didn't have stove fuel so I walked all the
way to Superette Mayra on the other side of
town. They didn't have stove fuel either.
But they did have charcoal so I bought a bag
of that instead.

While I was in line at the grocery store, I
met a real nice lady who told me about the

fresh fruit market on Fridays and Tuesdays.
And she also told me the taxis would take me
all the way back to my campsite for only $3.
So I didn't have to walk back with all my
groceries. I had heavy jugs of water and a
lot of food and a giant bag of charcoal. I
was able to get a fire started and make some
rice and carrots.

After dinner, I organized my pack and went
swimming. I stayed in the water for a
long time. I just sort of floated around
and looked up at the sky. The sand at
Flamenco Beach is soft. It's like a fine
powder. And the water is like the inside
of a swimming pool. It's calm and warm. I
have never been in a place like this before.
Maybe it's the constant sound of ocean waves
or the fact that my sleep schedule is in
sync with the sun. Maybe it's because I
haven't had any alcohol in a few days. But
there is something very beautiful about
this place. Doug and Lisa both work in the
restaurant industry but they were able to
get Monday off so they are going to come and
camp with me on Monday. Hopefully, we'll
go snorkeling together and spot some sea
turtles.

DAY 90 - Sunday, August 24 - [8:34pm]

Carlos Rosario Beach is the forbidden beach
that's fenced off by the military and
surrounded by explosives. To get there I
had to squeeze between a fence and a sign
that said, "Danger. Explosives. Do not
enter. No trespassing." So I squeezed
under the fence with all my gear. Then I
followed a trail all the way to the top of a
hill and then down the other side. I knew
all about this beach because I researched
it online. At one time, Culebra was used
as a military testing site. It's really
important to stay on the trail because there
are still live explosives around the island.
And if you step in the wrong place you could
blow yourself up. There are still stories
in the news here about old explosives being
found or exploded around the island.

So, finally, I get over to the other side of
the island to Carlos Rosario Beach. This is
the best snorkeling beach in all of Puerto
Rico. The coral comes almost all the way to
the surface even as the water gets to be 50
or 60 feet deep. And the sun lights up the
whole bay and brings out the most beautiful
orange and purple colors. And there are
giant tropical fish swimming around like
living rainbows. I swam so far out that
eventually some guy on a boat started waving
me over to him. He thought I was part of

his open ocean snorkeling tour group. He
kept blowing his whistle and waving me in.
I pointed towards the shore. He looked at
me like I was crazy.

DAY 91 - Monday, August 25 - [12:15am]

Earlier tonight, Doug and Lisa arrived. I
helped them put up their tent and Lisa
made drinks. I didn't feel like drinking.
Eileen, I don't feel like drinking ever
again. I know there are weird undertones
in my letters to you that sort of imply
alcoholism. That isn't by accident. And
the other night, the karaoke bar was enough
for me. I thankfully declined when Lisa
handed me a drink.

Doug made more drinks and blasted the radio.
I kept asking them to turn it down because
the other campers were trying to sleep. I
told them about the roosters that wake
everybody up at 6am but they didn't seem to
care. The two of them were yelling over the
radio. Doug made a fire. He was smacking
branches against a palm tree to break it
up for firewood. He was making a lot of
commotion. Lisa laughed loudly throughout
the night and screamed bloody murder when
she saw a bug in her tent.

DAY 92 - Tuesday, August 26 - [8:15pm]

Eileen, I took a shower! It was an amazing
shower! The place was infested with bees
and they swarmed around me the entire time.
There were hundreds of them. But I just
splashed them and they didn't sting me. I
feel fresh and smell like soap! I even put
on clean clothes. And then I made a very
tiny campfire and boiled water for tea.
Also, today I saw an iguana. It came right
up to me and my tent. Iguanas look like
small dinosaurs.

This morning, Doug and Lisa drank rum and
warm beer for breakfast. We went swimming
for a while and then made lunch. They had
to catch the afternoon ferry back and I
helped them pack up their tent. Doug was
nice enough to leave me some food and a
hammock and a little bug zapper that looks
like a tennis racket. I went into town with
them and we had dinner at the Dingy Dock
before they headed back to San Juan.

And now I am sipping green tea in a clean
tent with clean clothes.

DAY 93 - Wednesday, August 27 - [9:20pm]

Hi Eileen,
I still haven't seen any sea turtles. This

morning I went snorkeling at the very far
end of Flamenco Beach. It was nice but
challenging because the waves were getting
huge and the coral is like a maze over
there. I had to be very careful and it took
me a few tries to find a safe way back to
shore.

I spent most of the afternoon laying in
the hammock and reading a book about
optimism. Optimists seek change when things
aren't going well. Pessimists stay in bad
situations no matter how painful because
they don't believe there is a better way. I
want to be more of an optimist. I want to
run full speed after the things that make
me happy. Speaking of being happy. I've
discovered that coconuts make me happy. I
really like them. The green ones have the
most juice.

Also, today, I went for a walk and saw 3
iguanas. I followed them and they led me
to a fresh water lagoon where there were
iguanas everywhere! They were in the
trees, laying on the rocks, swimming in
the water – just everywhere. I stood there
watching them all for a while. Culebra is a
magical place, Eileen. You should come here
sometime.

DAY 94 - Thursday, August 28 - [9:54pm]

Hi Eileen.
There are a few mourning doves here.
Whenever I hear them coo it reminds me of
my parents' backyard. I grew up poor. I
never thought I'd make it as a writer in
Brooklyn. I never thought I'd be staying on
a beautiful beach for two weeks. When I was
a kid, I wasn't even allowed to leave the
backyard. We lived in a bad neighborhood.

Tonight I watched the sun set behind the
trees and it shot blue and purple rays all
across the clouds and lit up the beach in
this deep golden light. And the best view
of the sunset is in the water so I dove in
and watched the sky move and dance as the
sun gave one final light show before saying
goodnight. Even after the sun is set, the
water is warm and lovely. It's no wonder
why people love this place. The sand on
Flamenco Beach is so soft and you can wade
out 40 or 50 feet from the shore and still
touch the bottom. I just floated on my back
in that turquoise water and watched the sky
change colors. And when it got dark enough,
I walked back to my tent and brushed my
teeth on the beach.

I watched the moon come up and the stars
come into focus. And out in the ocean, way
out in the distance, was a giant cruise

ship all lit up like a birthday cake. I
had noticed it earlier in the day. But now
that it was dark and the sky blended into
the sea, that cruise ship looked like a
little floating city. There were probably
more people on that boat than there were on
Culebra. I felt like yelling out to them,
"There's no point in going anywhere else!
Flamenco Beach is heaven!"

DAY 95 - Friday, August 29 - [9:37pm]

This morning I woke up at 5:45AM and headed
for Carlos Rosario Beach. Eileen, I must
see some sea turtles on this trip. It was
one of the reasons I came here. I told
Jake that I was going to Puerto Rico to
swim with sea turtles so for some reason
it feels important to me. I grabbed my
snorkeling gear and snuck through the fence
and headed up the explosive trail again.
There was morning dew on the plants and the
air was still cool. I was definitely the
first one to walk the trail. I knew this
because there were a few spider webs across
the path. As I walked up the hill, I saw 3
deer standing at the top watching me. We
stood there looking at each other for a
moment. Then they ran up the hillside and
were gone. I worried about those deer not
sticking to the trail. I wondered how often

a deer sets off an explosive and gets blown
to smithereens.

I got to the beach and snorkeled around
for a while but saw no sea turtles. I ate
some food and went out again but still no
luck. Maybe it isn't sea turtle season.
Maybe they only come at certain times a
year. I walked back down the trail and over
to Flamenco Beach to do some snorkeling
there. This time I found a better spot to
enter between two rows of black rocks. It
was very beautiful and I saw many schools
of fish but no sea turtles. I went back to
my campsite and decided to start a little
campfire so I could make oatmeal.

After lunch, I headed back to Carlos Rosario
Beach to try again with the sea turtles.
Halfway there I discovered that I was almost
out of sunscreen. This is very dangerous
for me. I burn very easily. I didn't
have much water left either. And the only
kiosko on the beach that sells sunscreen
and gallons of water has been closed for two
days. I thought maybe I should take a break
from snorkeling and make my way into town
to get supplies. I felt very frustrated.
I had no sunscreen, almost no water and I
hadn't seen a sea turtle yet. I stood there
in the parking lot with all of my snorkel
gear. My tent and the grocery store were in
two different directions. And I didn't feel

like walking with all my gear all the way into town and back. I was standing in the parking lot deciding what to do when some guy said, "Taxi?"

I got in. Within 10 minutes I had water, sunscreen, chips, beans, pineapple slices, a candy bar and more potato chips. It was good luck meeting that taxi driver in the parking lot at the beach. Now I just had to get all this stuff back to my campsite. The second I walked out of the grocery store some guy said, "Do you need a ride?" "Hell yes." I got in his little golf cart. He was a gay man named Christopher from Tennessee. It was his 6th time staying at the Culebra International Hostel. When he noticed all my snorkeling gear, he told me about all his favorite beaches. "The sea turtles are on Tamarino Grand," he said. "Wait, what?" I said. "Yeah, right over there," he pointed as he drove the golf cart along the winding road. "Take that road by the yellow house, follow that down to the beach. Take a left on the beach and swim out towards the point. You want to get there early. The sea turtles are always there in the mornings."

I don't know if this guy was full of shit or not but I'm going to wake up early tomorrow and go find out.

DAY 96 - Saturday, August 30 - [8:34pm]

Sea turtles EVERYWHERE - gliding through the
shallow depths of these turquoise waters,
welcoming me into their blue silent movie as
they munched on ocean grass and floated up
to the surface for a calm, sweet breath. I
followed them out into the open ocean and
swam further than I probably should have.
I glided through the water with them for
hours.

Jake would have loved it. It was just me
and the sea turtles. Some of them were over
5 feet long.

By the time afternoon came, there were a
lot of tourists arriving. They piled out
of their rental cars with waterproof selfie
sticks. Most of the turtles headed out
to sea and I walked back to my tent. By
the time I got back, I was sunburned on my
back, calves and neck. But I didn't give
one damn about that. I slathered more
sunscreen on and hiked back over to Carlos
Rosario. I munched on some sunflower seeds
and dried fruit. I snorkeled around for
a while longer. I did a lot of thinking
over on that beach. I did not come to any
conclusions. I may have a hard time leaving
this place. I've fallen into a rhythm here.
There is a dance that happens with the doves
and the land crabs and the moonlit nights

and the chickens that wander around. I
know what time the mosquitos come out and
I know what time the birds start chirping.
Sometimes I take cover before the rain cloud
lets loose. The other day I saw that hermit
crab with the blue spotted shell and he
was just scrapping along doing his thing.
There are creatures flourishing in every
direction.

DAY 97 - Sunday, August 31 - [9:44pm]

Eileen, tonight there is a full moon. And
here I am camping on the ocean with a little
fire and a cup of green tea watching all
these giant waves crash into the shore.
The moon just lights up everything. It's
so bright the whole island is dancing in
moonlight. The palm leaves are swaying and
casting shadows in the sand. And I didn't
feel like sleeping. I don't want to leave
this place. I only have three days left. I
want to stay up all night just to experience
the island. I've been sitting on the beach
and watching the waves crash for hours.
Earlier in the day, I went snorkeling and
saw a squid and another barracuda. I
snorkeled all morning until that tour boat
showed up again and started waving me in.

DAY 98 - Monday, September 1 - [9:02pm]

Tonight was very strange. The moon cycle
was different than usual. Somehow the sun
completely set before the moon came up. On
past nights, I could step outside my tent
in the dead of night and see fairly well. I
am normally able to wander in the moonlight
and find a good place to pee. But tonight
I went outside and everything was black. It
was impossible to see. I was very startled
by this. I looked up into the sky and
there were stars everywhere. But there was
absolutely no moon light. I had to shine my
flashlight just to see where I was going.
Afterward, I sat on the beach and just
watched all the stars. I had never seen
anything like it before. So many bright
stars and I could see billions of them.
They went in all directions for all of
eternity. I looked at them for a long time.
And I got the sensation that I could fly up
there pretty easily.

DAY 98 - Monday, September 1 - [10:15pm]

Now the moon is up! The moon has risen and
it is lighting up the whole island again. I
guess it was just late tonight. This island
is very magical!

DAY 99 - Tuesday, September 2 - [9:08pm]

Hi Eileen, tomorrow is my last day on the
island. After tomorrow I will stop writing
you. I can't believe it's going to be
over. I've really enjoyed writing you. I
will miss you. I feel like there is so much
more I want to tell you. I guess that's
what being a writer is about - the strong
urge to share ideas. Maybe that's how you
feel about acting. I want you to know that
I'll be thinking about you and wishing great
fortune and success on your journey. Keep
faith when things don't look so good. Even
if things seem to be horrible, believe that
you will be okay and you will be. Bad moods
can pull you straight towards destruction
like a bad gust of wind when your kite is
too close to the ground. Don't worry about
the things that make you feel like shit.
Don't worry about those tough nights you
face in a hotel room alone. Concentrate on
what you want to feel. Focus on the things
you want to happen and you will soar to the
heavens.

DAY 100 - Wednesday, September 3 - [3:12pm]

Today went by very fast and I had to rush
into town to catch the ferry. I didn't want
to do it. I wanted to stay in my hammock
for another year. I went for one final swim

this morning and then had to pack quickly.
I rolled up my sleeping bag and fed my
remaining food to the chickens. I packed
all of my supplies (cooking gear, snorkel,
fins, tent, flashlight, knife, etc.) and
organized it in my bag. I walked the length
of Flamenco Beach, jumped in a cab and made
it to the ferry on time. I'm on the boat
now, writing these last few pages to you.
When we get back to the main island, I have
to take another cab and go directly to the
airport to catch my flight. I'll write you
when I'm on the plane.

DAY 100 - Wednesday, September 3 - [6:29pm]

Hi Eileen,
I am sitting at the airport right now and
something happened. Do you remember when
Jake told me about the whale sharks in Isla
Mujeres, Mexico? Remember he said they come
up to the surface and don't mind sharing the
water with a few humans?

Well, I was sitting in the airport with
my bag and all my snorkel gear thinking
about those giant whale sharks. They are
the biggest sharks in the ocean - gentle
creatures that are even bigger than my
apartment in Brooklyn. I didn't even think
about it. I just went up to the lady at

the counter and asked if I could change my
destination to Mexico. And when she told me
how much it would cost, I said, "Okay, book
it."

And Eileen, now I can't stop smiling! I
feel like I'm on the trapeze with you. I
feel like I'm soaring through the air and
I'm not sure if there is a net under us but
I don't care. I feel like running around
the airport giving high fives to people. I
don't care if they're strangers. We're all
just humans and when something good happens,
we should share it, Eileen.

But I have to tell you something. When
the lady at the counter handed me my new
boarding pass - my ticket to Mexico where
I'll soon be swimming with whale sharks -
the first person I wanted to tell was you.

DAY 100 - Wednesday, September 3 - [8:08pm]

Okay, I'm on the plane now. I even booked
my hotel from my phone while I was waiting.
I'm really going to miss you, Eileen. I
unfollowed you on Instagram so people don't
read this and come looking for you. I'll
miss your acrobatic pictures and your witty
comments. I'll miss your strange posts
about breakfast foods and acting gigs. And
I'll even miss the photos you take in the

morning when you think your hair looks funny
but really it looks fine.

I guess that's it. I hope you like this
book. I know this is all pretty strange
since we have never met. But I have a
feeling about you. And I keep trying to
remind myself that even our best friends
were once strangers.

OTHER BOOKS BY MARKUS ALMOND:

44162181R10062